Coming On Home Soon

Jacqueline
Woodson

Illustrated by
E. B. Lewis

G. P. PUTNAM'S SONS · NEW YORK

Published simultaneously in Canada. Manufactured in China by South China Printing Co. Ltd.

Designed by Cecilia Yung and Gunta Alexander. Text set in Arrus.

The art was done in watercolor on Arches paper.

Library of Congress Cataloging-in-Publication Data

Woodson, Jacqueline.

Coming on home soon / Jacqueline Woodson ; illustrated by E. B. Lewis. p. cm.

Summary: Staying with Grandma while Mama takes a job in Chicago during World War II, Ada Ruth
misses her mother, who loves her more than rain and snow. [1. Separation (Psychology)—Fiction.
2. Mother and child—Fiction. 3. Grandmothers—Fiction. 4. African Americans—Fiction.
5. World War, 1939–1945—United States—Fiction.] I. Lewis, Earl B., ill. II. Title.

PZ7.W868Co 2004   [E]—dc22   2003021949   ISBN 0-399-23748-8

1 3 5 7 9 10 8 6 4 2

First Impression

*For my aunts—Ada, Alicia and Ann
and, of course, for Toshi*
—J. W.

To the men and women at war, far from home
—E. B. L.

Mama's hands are warm and soft.
When she put her Sunday dress into the satchel, I held
   my breath.
Tried hard not to cry.
Ada Ruth, she said. *They're hiring colored women in Chicago since
   all the men are off fighting in the war.*
Mama folded another dress and put it in the bag.
I'm gonna head on up there.

Then she pulled me close up to her, pressed her face
    against mine.
Make some money I can send on home to you.

Outside, a pretty rain fell, making the brown fields shine.
Ada Ruth, Mama said. *Do you know I love you more than anything
    in the world?*
Yes, ma'am, I whispered. *More than rain.*
More than snow, Mama whispered back, the way we'd done
    a hundred times before.
Or maybe a hundred thousand.

Grandma holds me when I cry.

Hush now, she says. *It's going to be all right.*

Hush now, she says. *Your mama's gonna be coming on home soon.*

But Mama's been gone a long time. With no letter or money
   from her coming.

Keep writing to her, Grandma says.

So I do.

There is snow this morning.
And a small black kitten scratching against our door.
There is milk this morning, warm from the cow.
Grandma says, *You know we can't keep it.*
Then pours milk into a saucer and sets it down on the floor.

There is a war going on.
Some days not much food to speak of.
Corn bread and clabber milk for morning meal and supper.

You know we can't keep it, Grandma says again.
The kitten drinks the milk up,
rubs against my leg like it wants some more.
And Grandma says,
Don't go getting attached now, Ada Ruth.

It's a slip of a thing. But its softness is big.
And warm as ten quilts on my lap.
Warm as Mama's hands. I rub the kitten's back.
More than snow, Mama said.
I love you more than snow.
I watch the snow come down fast.
Try hard to remember the way my mama smelled.
Like sugar some days. And some days like sun.
Some days like the lye soap that turned her hands yellow
but got the wash real clean.

    I blink hard, but the tears
    still try to come.

Good thing it's too cold for fleas, Grandma says, coming in with
     more wood for the stove.
Or else that thing would be full of them.
She holds her head sideways, takes the kitten in.
Can't get much uglier now, can it?

Me and the kitten give Grandma a mean look.

Time passes.

When the postman goes on by without stopping, Grandma says,
Hush now. Don't start that crying.
But her eyes are sad.
Like she's wanting to cry too.

In Chicago, Mama said, *I can wash the railroad cars.*
Just imagine, Ada Ruth. A colored woman working on the railroad!

At night, me and Grandma listen to the radio,
hear about the battles being fought and all the men
who've died. I listen with my eyes closed,
pray for all those men who won't be coming on home soon.
Outside, the snow keeps falling.
The war goes on and on.

When Grandma turns the radio off, I rub my hand along
    the kitten's back
and think about the women working on the trains.
Just think.
My mama right there beside them.

Ice storm came last night, Grandma says
as she hunts possum and rabbit.
If she catches one, there'll be some meat for a stew.
A little bit of me hopes we find one.
A little bit of me hopes we don't.

Me and Grandma keep walking
and the kitten behind us, shivering until

Grandma stoops and lifts it into her coat.
Don't you know about cold snaps, she asks,
how they come on fast and sometimes stay?

The land goes on and on. Flat sometimes and then
   climbing up into a hill.

Grandma says it all leads out into the big, wide world.
One day I'm gonna set off to see it all.
Maybe I'll go by railroad.

When we get home, Grandma starts the woodstove going,
  our wet clothes steaming on top of it.
Hot cocoa too. And two biscuits from last night's supper.
And the postman making his way up the road.

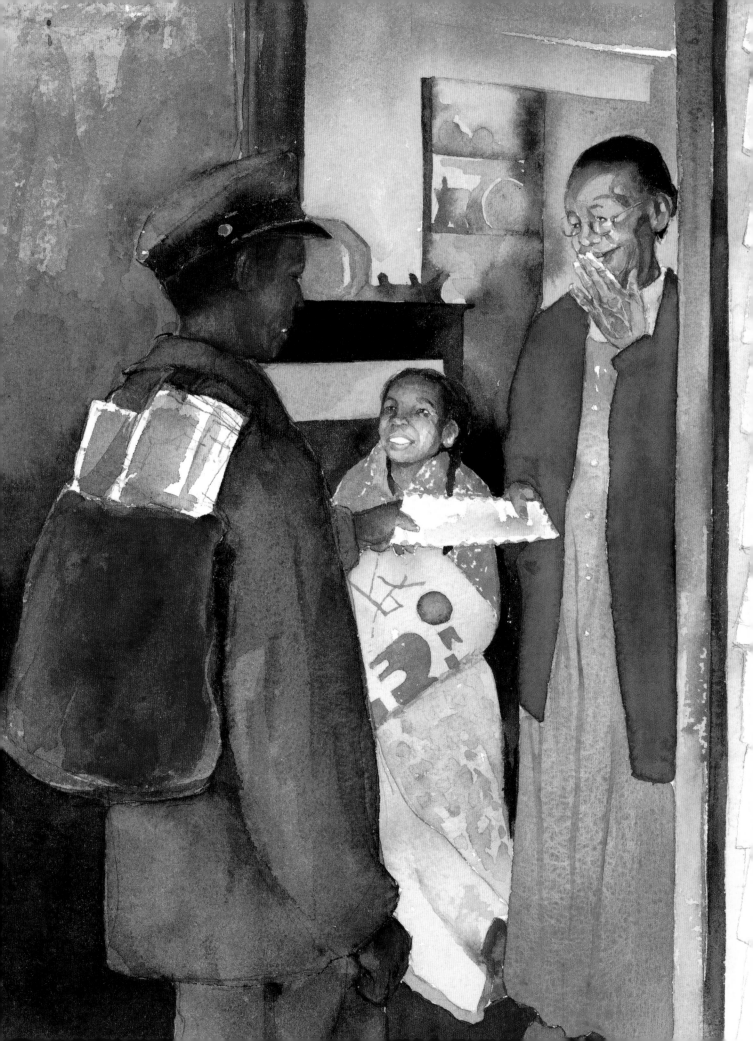

Thank you, Lord, Grandma whispers
when he puts the letter with Mama's beautiful cursive in her hand.
Money falling from it when Grandma steams it open and
    the first line—*Tell Ada Ruth*
I'll be coming on home soon—like a song you want to sing
    over and over.

The small black kitten beside us as we read the letter
  again and again.
I think she's taken a mind to stay, I say.
Well, she needs to take a mind to go, Grandma says.
But she puts a blanket down by the fire, and whispers,
Quiet and halfway pretty when you look at her in just the right way.

Inside, it's warm and quiet.
Stew cooking on the stove.
Outside, snow falls and falls
and somewhere there's my mama
loving me more than rain.
Loving me more than snow.
Cleaning trains.

And coming on home soon.